To Art and Steve, thanks for the HELP!
And to the tiny towns of Frostburg, College Hill, Mariemont,
and Terrace Park: you know how to put the LIGHTS ON!

About This Book

The illustrations for this book were digitally born with Adobe Fresco. This book was edited by Christy Ottaviano and designed by Patrick Hulse. The production was supervised by Kimberly Stella, and the production editor was Marisa Finkelstein. The text was set in Proxima Nova Soft, and the display types are Filson Soft and GoodDog New.

Little
Red

Will Hillenbrand

Christy Ottaviano Books
LITTLE, BROWN AND COMPANY
NEW YORK BOSTON

In a Tiny Town there was a Little Red Truck, whose driver was Katie. They never stopped working until the job was done.

Even when the snow started to fall.

"My engine won't start,"
honked Purple Delivery Van.

Little Red and Katie went right to work.
Jumper cables sure come in handy.

"Thanks for the jump,"
honked Purple Delivery Van.

"You got it!" tooted Little Red.
"See ya later!"

Honk, honk!
Beep, beep!

The snow came down.

Little Red had just
one more job for the day.

"I've got a busted headlight,"
whistled Blue Calliope Car.

Little Red and Katie
got busy with the repair.

"Much better. I can see now.
Thanks for the bulb,"
whistled Blue Calliope Car.

"Play on," tooted Little Red.
"See ya later!"

Honk, honk!
Beep, beep!

The snow came down and down.

But then he heard . . .

Help,
Little Red,
help!

"We're stuck,"
blared Green Fire Truck.

Little Red and Katie
knew what to do.

"Easy now, easy—just a little bump . . ."

"All set! Thanks for the push,"
blared Green Fire Truck.

"No problem," tooted Little Red.
"See ya later!"

Honk, honk!
Beep, beep!

The snow came down, down, and down.

Then he heard . . .

"I've got a flat tire,"
rang Yellow Popcorn Wagon.

Little Red and Katie got out
the jack and elevated the wheel.
Then they put on the spare.

"Thanks for the tire,"
rang Yellow Popcorn Wagon.

"Of course," tooted Little Red.
"See ya later!"

Honk, honk!
Beep, beep!

The snow came down, down, down,
and down.

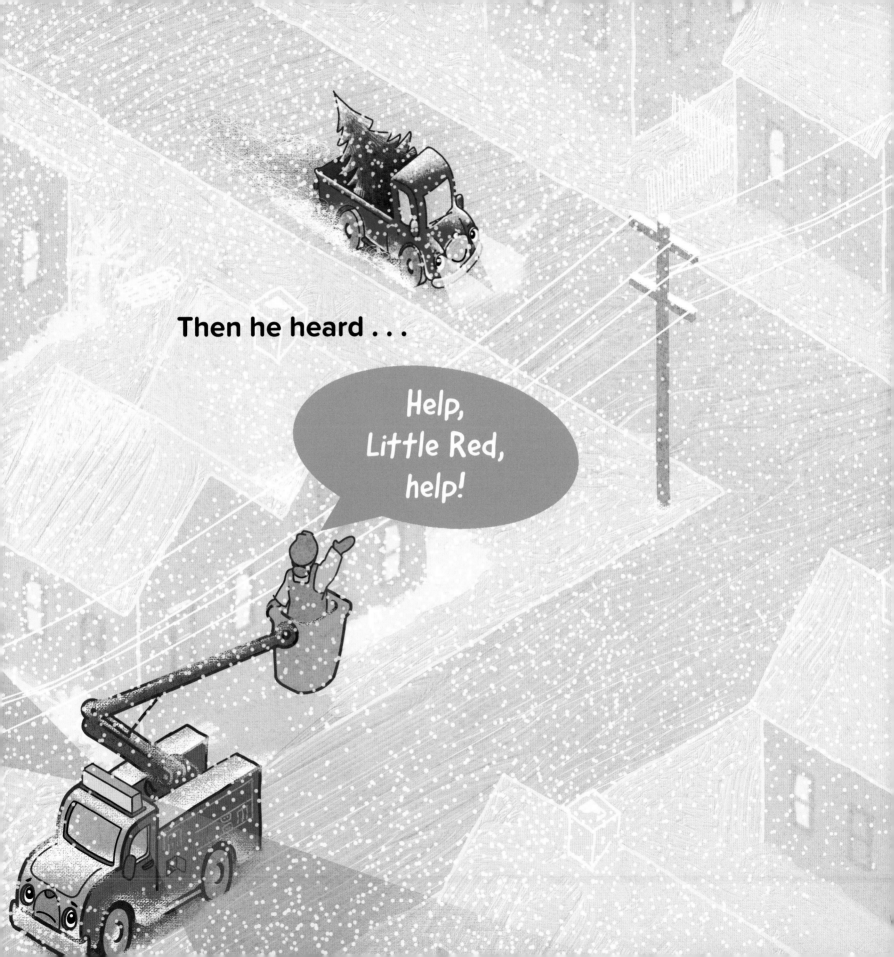

Then he heard . . .

Help, Little Red, help!

"We're out of gas!"
bellowed Orange Utility Truck.

Little Red and Katie didn't miss a beat.

"Thanks for the fuel,"
bellowed Orange Utility Truck.

"You bet," tooted Little Red.
"See ya later!"

Honk, honk!
Beep, beep!

The snow came down, down, down,
down, and down.

Then he heard . . .

Help, Little Red, help!

"We've got a broken hitch!" jingled Shiny Silver Sleigh.

Little Red and Katie fixed the situation in no time.

"Thanks for the hitch,"
jingled Shiny Silver Sleigh.

"Away you go!" tooted Little Red.
"See ya later!"

Honk, honk!
Beep, beep . . .

"Phew, I think our day
is almost done."

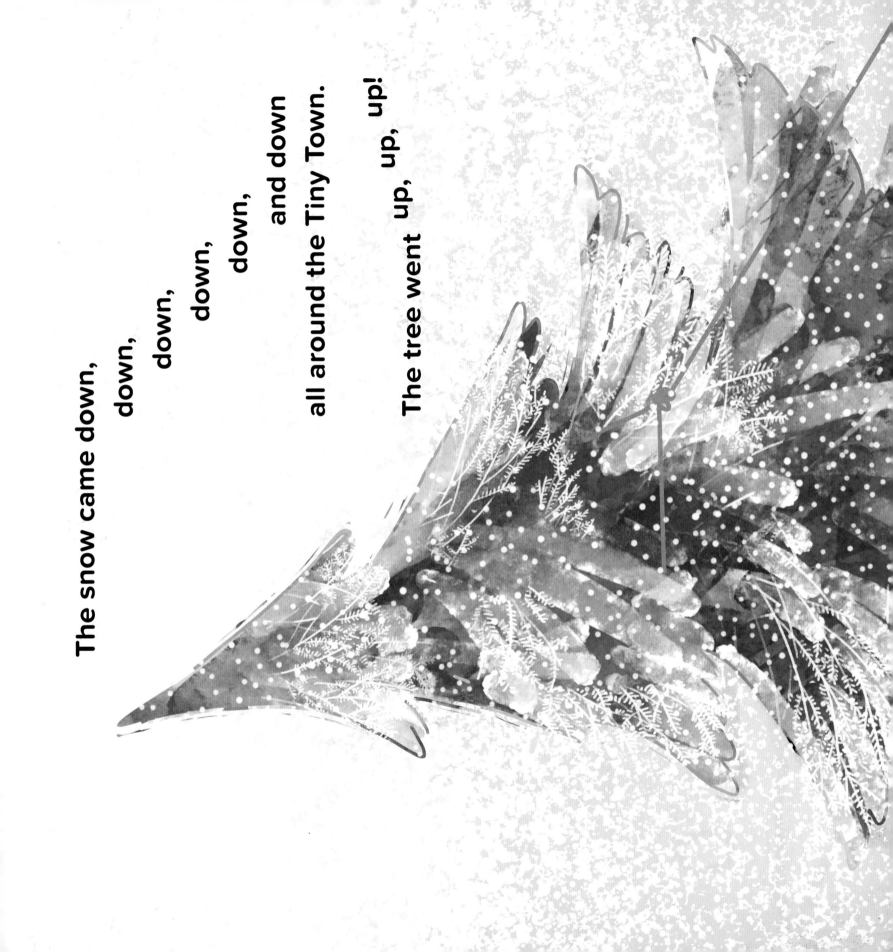

The snow came down,
down,
down,
down,
down,
and down
all around the Tiny Town.

The tree went up, up, up, up!

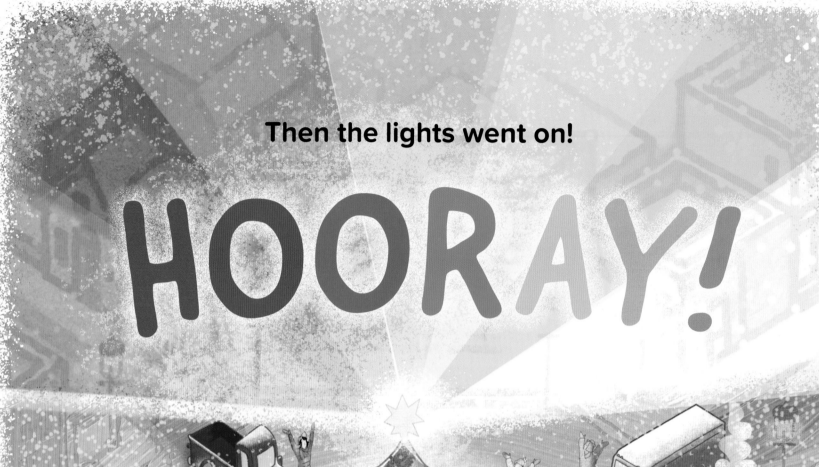

Then the lights went on!

HOORAY!